LOEK KOOPMANS

Frog, Bee and Look for Snow

Floris Books

Spring had arrived. It was time for Snail to wake up. He stretched his feelers in the warm sunlight.

A little bird landed nearby. "Oh, what a winter it's been!" the bird twittered. "I've never seen such snow falling! So deep, so cold, so white. I'm glad it's spring again."

Before Snail could say anything, the bird had flown away. Snail began to wonder. Snow falling? Deep, cold, white? What was the little bird talking about?

Snail looked around his green world. He looked up at the sky. Where could this snow be falling from?

Just then his friend Bee appeared. "Good morning, Bee," said Snail. "A little bird just told me about deep, cold, white snow falling this winter. Do you know anything about snow?"

Bee had no idea, for she had spent all winter in her hive. "I'll go and ask my flying friends. I'll be back soon," she said, taking off.

Bee asked all sorts of flying creatures. "Do you know anything about snow? Where does it came from? Does falling snow hurt when it hits you on the head?"

The flying creatures didn't have any answers. Butterfly had been hiding all winter. Bird had just returned from her journey south, and the other animals had just woken up from their winter sleep. They had never seen snow.

Bee was none the wiser.

A little later, Snail happened to meet his friend Frog who was lying in a pond enjoying the spring sun. "Good morning, Frog," said Snail. "A little bird just told me about deep, cold white snow falling this winter. Do you know anything about snow?"

Frog had no idea, for he had
stayed all winter deep down in the
mud. "I'll go and ask my watery
friends. I'll be back soon," he said,
disappearing under the water.

Frog asked all sorts of pond
creatures. "Do you know anything
about snow? Where does it come
from? Does falling snow hurt when
it hits you on the head?"

The watery creatures didn't
have any answers. All of them
stayed deep down in the pond all
winter. They had never seen snow.

Frog was none the wiser.

When the three friends met later, Snail said to them: "Frog, you live in water, and Bee, you live in the sky. And I live on the earth. Between us, we should know everything about the world! So why don't we know anything about deep cold white snow?"

"I think," he added, "that we must go and look for snow."

"Yes!" said Frog and Bee. And so the three friends set off on a journey to look for snow.

They travelled slowly because Snail
could not go very fast. Before they
knew it, springtime had turned
quietly into summer.

One warm sunny day, they came to some
tall giant sunflowers. Bee flew up to
speak to one of them. "Hello sunflower,"
she said. "We're on our way to find some
falling snow. Do you know about deep
cold white snow?"

Sunflower didn't have any answers.
Her huge flower head only came out in
the warmth of the summer. She had never
seen snow.

"Never mind," said Bee, though she was
quite disappointed. Frog, Bee and Snail
wandered through a beautiful world. They
went to places they had never been before.
Wherever they went, they asked about snow.

The summer plants didn't have any answers.
They had just sprouted from their seeds. They
had never seen snow.

Sadly, the three friends travelled on, day
after day. The friends were now a long way
from home. For many weeks they had travelled
along valleys and over hills, and now it was
autumn. Frog, Bee and Snail were quite tired
when they arrived at a wood. The trees were
bright with autumn leaves.

"Let's ask the trees," said Snail hopefully.
The trees didn't have any answers. In fact,
they didn't answer at all.
"I am afraid we will never find snow,"
said Bee very quietly. The three friends sat
down. They were beginning to lose hope.

The sun slowly faded behind the trees.
A cold wind blew from the north.
    Frog, Bee and Snail took shelter under
the autumn leaves.

Poor Snail, he was so tired. Poor Bee, she was so hungry. Poor Frog, he was so cold. They had come such a long way to look for snow and they were exhausted. They crept further beneath the leaves and fell into a deep sleep.

They woke the next morning to find
a strange and wonderful world. It was
winter and white flakes were falling
softly from the sky. A deep white
blanket had covered the earth.

Frog, Bee and Snail had never seen anything like it. They were afraid at first, but then they understood. It was deep. It was cold. It was white. Snow! Falling snow.

Twirling snowflakes landed on their heads and they didn't hurt. Frog, Bee and Snail were proud and happy.

However, the snow was very cold, much too cold for the friends. They needed help.

"Please, help us. Is there anybody who can help us?" they cried out.

No answer came from the silent wood. But
listen ...! From deep down in the earth
came a gentle rumble which grew louder
and louder. Suddenly the snow burst open.
Two helping hands appeared.
 The hands gently enclosed the three
friends and protected them from the cold.

The helping hands belonged to Mother Nature. She picked the friends up and said: "My dear Frog, Bee and Snail. You have been very brave coming so far north, but you need a muddy ditch, your hive and a quiet spot to rest for the winter. I will take you home."

With a few strides they left the cold
north and came to the warm south
where she placed them gently back on
the earth.

Frog, Bee and Snail thanked Mother
Nature and within moments fell into a
deep, deep sleep.

Do you know what they dreamed about?
Deep, cold, white snow.